A thousand thanks to Jean-Pïerre Baillet, E.T.

Text copyright © 2004 by Brigitte Weninger
Illustrations copyright © 2004 by Eve Tharlet
Coproduction with Michael Neugebauer Publishing Ltd. Hong Kong
Published simultaneously in Canada.
Manufactured in Hong Kong by Wide World Ltd.
Designed by Michael Neugebauer
Typesetting in Icone
Color separation by Fotoreproduzioni Grafiche, Verona, Italy.

Library of Congress Cataloging-in-Publication Data available upon
request.
ISBN 0-698-40006-2
10 9 8 7 6 5 4 3 2 1
First Impression

For more information please visit our website: www.minedition.com

a minedition book
published by Penguin Young Readers Group

A Child Is a Child

Brigitte Weninger

Illustrated by Eve Tharlet

Translated by Charise Myngheer

"Ribbiiiiitt…Ribbiiiiitt! When is dad coming home?"
"I don't know," croaked Mama Frog, worried.
"I think I'll go look for him. Be good while I am gone."
Mama Frog blew them a kiss and hopped off.
The two little frogs waited and waited, but Mama
and Daddy Frog never came home.

"Rib-biit! Rib-biiiiitt! Rib-biiiiitt!"
Mrs. Blackbird, Mr. Mole and Mr. Hedgehog heard the little
frogs crying.

"What's wrong?" they asked.

Bit by bit they heard the sad story.
"Hmmmm, this is really a terrible thing," they all thought.

"What should we do?" asked Mrs. Blackbird.
"Little frogs can't live in a bird's nest."
"No," said Mr. Mole. "That doesn't work. But my dark
  hole isn't a good place either."
"And I'm always on the move," said Mr. Hedgehog.
"How could I take care of two little frogs?"

"Rib-ibiit! Rib-biiiiitt! Rib-biiiiitt!"
Mama Mouse came scurrying towards them, with five
tiny mice hanging onto her tail.
"Oh, my, why so many tears?" she asked.
She quickly picked up two soft leaves to wipe their eyes.

"The two little frogs are all alone," said Mr. Hedgehog.
"We feel sorry for them, but none of us can keep them.
 Maybe there is a frog pond where someone else
 could take care of them."
 Mama Mouse hugged the two little frogs.
"We'll take them," she said.

"Hmmmft," snorted Mr. Hedgehog. "I know you mean well.
Maybe you should think it over. A frog is not a mouse or
a mole or a blackbird. Frogs need completely different things
than we do!
It's just not that easy…"

"That's ridiculous!" cried Mama Mouse.
"It's simple. A child is a child. All children
  need a place to live and play,
  good food to eat and someone
  who loves them!"
"Hurray!" peeped the tiny mice.
"The little frogs get to stay with us!
  Now we can play together.
  And Mama will fix us pudding!"

"Pudding!" cried Mr. Hedgehog. "But frogs eat insects and worms like me!"

"Good then," smiled Mama Mouse. "Please find a couple of juicy worms for our sweet little frogs. And for dessert, they get pudding! It will be fun for them to try something new!"

Mr. Hedgehog looked doubtful, but he scampered off to start his search.

"In the meantime, Mr. Mole can dig our little frogs a bedroom.
There's nobody better or faster than him!"
Mr. Mole proudly agreed. "Of course! I'll start right away!" he said.
"And Mrs. Blackbird could look for a bathtub. Our little
frogs will need a waterbed!"

Everyone went right to work. Mr. Mole dug a roomy bedroom for the sweet little frogs. Mr. Hedgehog served them delicious worms. And Mrs. Blackbird found them a beautiful bathtub to sleep in. "So Mama Mouse," chimed her friends. "Now you have seven wonderful children to take care of, but we're all here to help you!"

"Rib-bit-peep! Rib-bit-peep!"
There was a lot for Mama Mouse and her friends to do. But
the little frogs soon learned to peep and scamper. And the tiny mice
learned to ribbit and swim.
"What did I tell you?" said Mama Mouse contently.
"We're completely different, but…"

"A CHILD IS A CHILD.
  It's just that simple!"